Rebecca
the Rock 'n' Roll Fairy

by Daisy Meadows

LITTLE APPLE

SCHOLASTIC INC.

New York   Toronto   London   Auckland   Sydney
Mexico City   New Delhi   Hong Kong   Buenos Aires

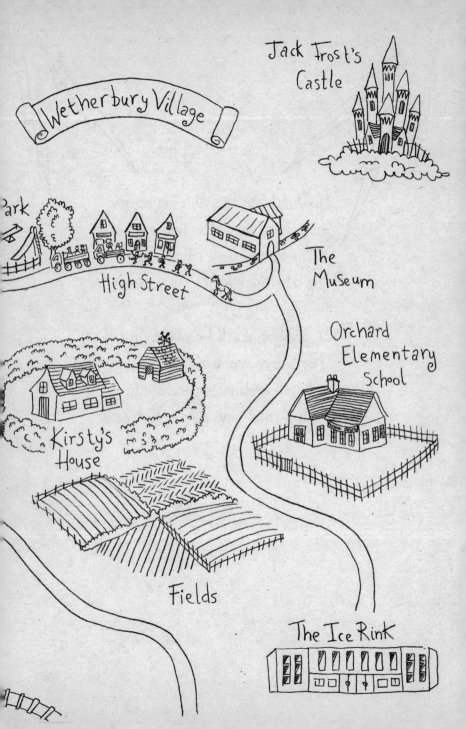

Hold tight to the ribbons, please.
You goblins may now feel a breeze.
I'm summoning a hurricane
To take the ribbons away again.

But, goblins, you'll be swept up too,
For I have work for you to do.
Guard each ribbon carefully,
By using your new power to freeze.

Contents

Rock 'n' Roll Party

"Are you ready yet, Mom?" Kirsty Tate called up the stairs. "Rachel and I are dying to see your costumes!" She grinned at her best friend, Rachel Walker, who was standing next to her.

"We'll be down soon," Mrs. Tate called back from the bedroom.

Kirsty and Rachel sat down on the bottom stair to wait.

"I wish we were going to the rock 'n' roll party with my mom and dad." Kirsty sighed. "It sounds like fun, *and* we might find Rebecca the Rock 'n' Roll Fairy's magic ribbon there!"

Rachel nodded. "The Dance Fairies are depending on us," she reminded Kirsty. Rachel and Kirsty had become friends with the fairies during their vacation on

Rainspell Island, and now the girls were always eager to help whenever the fairies had a problem.

The main cause of trouble in Fairyland was mean Jack Frost and his goblins. A few days earlier, Jack Frost had asked the Dance Fairies to visit his ice castle and teach his goblins how to dance. But it was all a trick, so the goblins could steal the Dance Fairies' magic ribbons!

When the king and queen of Fairyland had demanded that Jack Frost give the ribbons back, he refused. Instead, he sent seven of his goblins tumbling into the human world, each clutching one of the ribbons. Now, during their school break, Kirsty and Rachel were helping the Dance Fairies find their ribbons.

"We've gotten off to a good start," Kirsty remarked. "We already found Bethany the Ballet Fairy's ribbon, and Jade the Disco Fairy's, too."

"But if we don't find the rest, all the other kinds of dance will keep going wrong, and dancing won't be fun anymore!" Rachel sighed.

"Yes, and I guess the dancing at the rock 'n' roll party tonight will be ruined, since Rebecca's rock 'n' roll ribbon is still missing," Kirsty replied with a worried frown. "Do you remember how Bethany told us that the magic ribbons are attracted to their own kind of dancing?"

Rachel asked. "Maybe the goblin who has Rebecca's ribbon will be at the rock 'n' roll party!"

"Girls, we're ready!" Mr. Tate yelled from upstairs, and Kirsty and Rachel turned around.

When Mr. and Mrs. Tate came downstairs, the girls' eyes widened with delight. Kirsty's dad was wearing jeans and a black leather jacket. Kirsty's mom was wearing a sleeveless black top and a full white skirt embroidered with black musical notes.

She wore a high ponytail tied with a red ribbon.

"You both look *fantastic!*" Kirsty gasped.

"You look like you just walked out of the movie *Grease!*" Rachel added. "Will everyone be dressed up like you?"

Mr. Tate nodded. "There will also be demonstrations of rock 'n' roll dancing," he explained, "and an Elvis impersonator. Elvis Presley was a famous rock 'n' roll singer, you know."

"And Kirsty's Uncle John is in charge of the music," Mrs. Tate told Rachel. "We're taking some of our own rock 'n' roll records for him to play."

"It sounds like fun," Kirsty said wistfully.

"Well, why don't you two come with us?" Mrs. Tate suggested with a smile. "We didn't ask you before because there aren't going to be any other kids there, but you might enjoy it."

Kirsty and Rachel looked thrilled.

"Can we?" Kirsty asked eagerly.

"But what about Gran? She was going to come and stay with us."

"She won't have left home yet," Mrs. Tate said, glancing at the clock. "I'll give her a call."

"Does it matter that we don't have costumes?" Rachel asked.

"Not at all," Mr. Tate assured her.

"Isn't this great?" Kirsty whispered to Rachel as they went to grab their coats.

"We're going to the rock 'n' roll party after all!"

"Yes, and maybe we'll find Rebecca's rock 'n' roll ribbon there!" Rachel replied excitedly.

Rebecca in a Spin

After Mrs. Tate had called Kirsty's grandma, they all set off for the village hall where the rock 'n' roll party was being held. As they walked inside and took off their coats, the girls looked around eagerly. Everyone was dressed in rock 'n' roll outfits, and rock music was playing in the background. There were

round tables and chairs set up,
with a large space in the
middle for dancing.
Kirsty also noticed a
refreshments table
with food and
drinks for sale. At
the opposite end
of the hall was a
brightly lit stage.

"Who's *that*?"
Rachel asked
curiously, pointing
to a man on the
stage who was busy
setting up a microphone.
The man had dark hair and
bushy sideburns, and he was
wearing a sparkly white jumpsuit.

"Oh, that's the Elvis impersonator," Mrs. Tate explained. "He'll be singing later on." "We'll pick up some drinks and snacks for everyone and then find a table," said Mr. Tate. "Would you girls mind taking these records to John? He's over there by the D.J. station." Mr. Tate handed the box of old records to Kirsty. He and Mrs. Tate went to join the line at the refreshments table.

Meanwhile, Rachel and Kirsty made their way across the hall. The record players were connected to some very large speakers next to the stage. Boxes of records had been set out in neat rows, but there was no sign of Kirsty's uncle.

"I wonder where Uncle John is," Kirsty remarked.

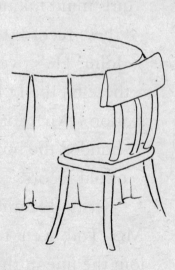

"I'm right here!" A blond man who looked a lot like Mr. Tate popped up from under the table. "I was just fixing a loose wire. How are you, Kirsty?"

"I'm fine, Uncle John." Kirsty grinned, handing over the box of records. "This is my friend Rachel."

"Ah, the famous Rachel!" Uncle John

exclaimed. "I've heard a lot about you! Excuse me for a moment, girls," he said quickly, "I need to get the next record ready to start."

Kirsty and Rachel watched as Uncle John put another record on one of the turntables.

"Ladies and gentlemen!" came an announcement. "May I have your

attention, please?" There was a burst of applause, and Kirsty and Rachel turned to see the Elvis impersonator on the stage. "I'd like to welcome you all to our rock 'n' roll party!" Elvis went on. "We have a fantastic night of entertainment lined up. First on stage are Linda and Will Melling, who are going to show us how to dance rock 'n' roll style."

As Linda and Will walked onto the stage in their sparkly early rock 'n' roll outfits, the girls exchanged a worried glance.

"I hope their dance goes OK without the magic ribbon," Kirsty whispered.

"My fingers are crossed!" Rachel whispered back.

Uncle John lowered the needle onto the record and the music began. The song had a very fast beat, and Linda and Will started by holding hands and doing lots of twists and turns around the stage.

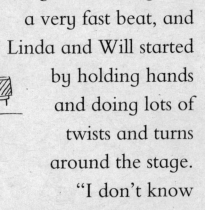

"I don't know anything about rock 'n' roll dancing, but this looks great to me!" Rachel said to Kirsty.

But at that very moment, Linda stumbled. She managed to regain her balance quickly and smiled brightly at the audience, but the next second Will tripped and stubbed his toes on the floor.

"Ow!" he yelped, looking embarrassed.

Linda tried to cover up the mistake by twirling across the stage in front of him. Unfortunately, she clumsily stepped on Will's other foot as she did!

"*Ouch!*" Will gasped.

"Oh no!" Kirsty groaned as Will and Linda tried to keep dancing, blushing furiously. "This is all because Rebecca's ribbon is missing!"

Rachel nodded. The girls watched anxiously, hoping nothing else would happen, but it soon became clear that Linda and Will had both forgotten their steps. Linda went left when she should have gone right, Will went right when he should have gone left, and they ended up slamming into each other. Then, Linda jumped into Will's arms and he tried to lift her above his head, but they fell in a tangled heap on the stage.

The audience looked shocked and the Elvis impersonator rushed out of the wings to help the dazed dancers to their feet. After the three whispered back and forth, Elvis grabbed the microphone again.

"Linda and Will are going to take a quick break," he announced, sounding kind of nervous. "They'll be back for another performance later."

Looking embarrassed, Linda and Will fled from the stage as everyone applauded politely. Kirsty and Rachel felt very sorry for them.

"I don't understand it!" Uncle John said in confusion, as he put another record on. "Linda and Will are usually amazing! Maybe one of them is feeling sick or something. I'll just go backstage and make sure they're OK." He slipped out from behind the turntables. "Will you girls keep an eye on things for me?" he asked. "I'll be back before this song is over."

The girls nodded and Uncle John rushed away.

"Poor Linda and Will," Kirsty said. "This is all because of mean Jack Frost and his goblins!"

"Hello!" called a tiny, silvery voice just then.

Rachel grabbed Kirsty's arm. "Did you hear that?"

Kirsty nodded. "But where's it coming from?" she asked, glancing around.

"I'm down here!" the voice called.

Rachel and Kirsty looked down at the record players. There, sitting on the edge of the record that was spinning around on the turntable, was a tiny, sparkling fairy.

"Oh!" Kirsty exclaimed. "It's Rebecca the Rock 'n' Roll Fairy!"

A Glimpse of Goblins

"Hi, girls!" called Rebecca, a smile spreading across her pretty face. She wore a purple scoop-necked shirt, a black skirt embroidered with big pink spots, and a matching pink scarf around her neck. Her long brown hair was tied up in a ponytail, just like Mrs. Tate's.

"Hi, Rebecca!" Rachel and Kirsty

whispered as the little fairy fluttered daintily off the spinning record.

"What are you doing here?" added Kirsty eagerly. "Is your ribbon close by?"

Rebecca nodded. "I think so," she said in a low voice. "I can feel it, but it can't be too close. Otherwise, poor Linda and Will wouldn't have danced so badly."

Rachel and Kirsty nodded. They knew that when a magic ribbon was very close by, everyone danced beautifully.

"Girls, we have to find the ribbon before Linda and Will go back on-stage," Rebecca said in a determined voice. "Then their rock 'n' roll dancing will be perfect! Will you help me look for the goblin? He must be around here *somewhere*."

"Of course we will," Kirsty replied. But just then she saw Uncle John heading back toward them. "Rebecca, here comes my uncle! You'd better hide."

Rebecca immediately flew to hide on Rachel's shoulder behind her hair.

"Looks like Will and Linda are fine now," Uncle John said cheerfully. "I just watched them practicing backstage, and they were wonderful! I think they must have had stage fright before."

"That's very strange!" Rebecca whispered to Rachel. "My ribbon's still missing, but Will and Linda are dancing well again. That can only mean one thing . . ."

". . . the ribbon's backstage!" Rachel finished in a low voice.

"Then let's go backstage right away, and find the goblin!" Kirsty whispered, excited.

There was a door

at the side of the stage and
the girls headed toward
it, leaving Uncle John
to put on another
record.

They were
worried that
someone might
notice them.
Luckily, people
were too busy
chatting and buying
refreshments. There were a lot of couples
already on the dance floor, including
Mr. and Mrs. Tate. But just like Will and
Linda, they all kept bumping into each
other, stepping on toes, and forgetting
their steps.

"This party will be a disaster if I don't find my ribbon soon!" Rebecca sighed as Kirsty opened the door.

Rebecca, Rachel, and Kirsty found Will and Linda practicing their routine in a room behind the stage. The two dancers seemed like a different couple from the clumsy, awkward duo who had performed earlier. Now their kicks and twirls were completely in time and they didn't make a single mistake.

"Uncle John

was right!" Kirsty said admiringly, as Will flipped Linda high into the air and caught her again. "They're amazing!"

"My ribbon is in here somewhere!" Rebecca said eagerly. "I can sense it!"

Rachel glanced around and suddenly noticed that one of the cabinet doors behind them stood slightly open. As she stared at it, she saw a knobby green foot poke through the opening, just for a second. Then it quickly disappeared again.

"Kirsty! Rebecca!" Rachel whispered excitedly. "There's a goblin inside that cabinet!"

Goblins Revealed!

"Are you sure?" Rebecca asked.

Rachel nodded. "I saw his foot poking out," she explained.

"We can't do anything about the goblin while Will and Linda are here," Kirsty said. "We'll have to wait until they're done practicing."

The girls watched as Will and Linda

worked on their finale. Will threw Linda
up into the air again, where she turned a
double-somersault and landed in Will's
arms. They smiled, and next Will helped
Linda drop into a split.

"That's much better!" Will exclaimed.
"I don't know *what* went wrong before."
"Yes, it was *so* embarrassing!" Linda
groaned.

"Let's get something to drink before we go back onstage," Will suggested. They hurried off, giving the girls a friendly wave as they left.

Immediately, Rebecca flew out from behind Rachel's hair. The three friends dashed over to the cabinet.

"Be careful, Kirsty!" Rachel warned as her friend reached for the door handle. "Remember that Jack Frost has given the goblins freezing powers!"

Carefully, Kirsty pulled the door open and the girls looked inside.

The cabinet was full of music stands, old props from plays, and *two* goblins squished one behind the other. The goblin in the front was holding a sparkly purple ribbon in his hand.

When they saw the girls, the goblins both let out loud grunts of annoyance.

"Go away!" yelled the one with the ribbon, trying to pull the door closed again. "You can't see us! We're hiding!"

The other one scowled, grabbed the head from a horse costume, and pulled it over his own head. "Now you really can't see me!" he said in a muffled voice. "Go away!"

But Kirsty shook her head firmly.

"I'm not going anywhere until I get my magic ribbon back!" Rebecca said, hovering in the doorway.

The first goblin looked nervous. "Don't come near me!" he shrieked. "I don't want to be frozen!"

Rachel, Kirsty, and Rebecca glanced at each other in confusion. "You fool!" the second goblin said, pulling the horse's head off and poking his friend in the ribs. "*We're* the ones who have the power to freeze people — as long as we have a magic ribbon!"

"Oh yes!" said the first goblin. "I forgot." Then his face darkened as he looked at his friend. "Don't you poke me, or I'll poke you harder!"

Rachel was staring at the second goblin. "That's the goblin who stole

Bethany's ballet ribbon!" she whispered
to Kirsty.

"I think he
recognized us,
too!" Kirsty
whispered back
as the second
goblin glared
at them.

"Never mind
me!" he yelled as
the first goblin gave
him a sharp poke in the ribs. "You
should be freezing the pesky fairy and her
human friends."

"Ooh, yes!" said the first goblin
eagerly.

"I'll turn you into fairies, girls,"
Rebecca called, quickly lifting her wand

as the first goblin jumped out of the cabinet at them. "Go on, freeze them all!" The second goblin snickered, tumbling out after his friend. A shower of magic dust from Rebecca's wand swirled around Rachel and Kirsty and transformed them into fairies in the twinkling of an eye. The girls fluttered their glittery wings and flew up into the air, out of the goblin's reach.

"Oh, I *hate* when they do that!" the first goblin said angrily. He started jumping up into the air, swatting at Rachel, Kirsty, and Rebecca. "Freeze!"

he shouted again and again, but he
missed every time.

"What do we do now?" Rachel asked
as they flew above the goblins' heads.
"We still have to get the ribbon back."

"It's going to be hard with two
goblins," Rebecca said anxiously.

Kirsty frowned at the two goblins
below. The first one was still leaping up
and down and shouting, "Freeze!" He

didn't seem to realize the fairies were well out of his reach.

"Maybe we could get the first goblin to freeze the second one?" she suggested. "We just have to make sure they're touching each other when the first goblin says 'Freeze!'"

"That's a great idea!" Rebecca said with a big grin. "Let's trick them into it. On the count of three — one, two, three!" Grabbing hands, Rachel, Kirsty, and Rebecca immediately flew down and hovered near the second goblin. With a cry of triumph, the first goblin rushed toward them. The girls waited until the last possible moment, and then zoomed up and out of reach.

"Freeze!" shouted the first goblin, just as he crashed into his friend.

The Magic Singing Stick

Instantly, the second goblin was frozen solid! The first goblin landed on the ground. His frozen friend fell over and landed in his lap. The first goblin looked so shocked, the girls and Rebecca couldn't help laughing.

"Oh no!" The first goblin groaned. He pushed his frozen friend off his lap so that

he could stand up. Then he stood the
second goblin up, too, and examined him
carefully. He poked and prodded
him. He even tried breathing warm air
onto him, but it was no use. The second
goblin remained completely frozen, with
an expression of surprise on his face.

"So now we only have one goblin to
deal with!" said Rebecca. "How will we
make him give my ribbon back?"

Before the girls could answer, they heard the sound of music coming from the stage behind them. The Elvis impersonator had started singing. The slow, beautiful melody filled the room.

"Oh!" Kirsty said suddenly, "I know this! It's a famous Elvis Presley song called *Love Me Tender*. My dad plays it all the time."

"I think the goblin likes it, too!" Rachel whispered.

The first goblin had stopped trying to thaw out his friend. Instead, he was swaying to the music, his head cocked to one side. There was a look of wonder on his face. "I've never heard such beautiful music!" he said with awe, waving the magic ribbon and beginning to dance.

"He can't help but dance to rock 'n' roll music while he's holding my ribbon." Rebecca laughed as the goblin danced his way closer to the entrance to the stage. "We'd better follow him, girls!"

"What about the frozen goblin?" asked Rachel. "We can't leave him here. Somebody might see him!"

Rebecca waved her wand. The frozen goblin rose into the air and gently floated

into the prop cabinet. Then the door
closed behind him. The other goblin was
now standing in the wings, still swaying
dreamily and watching the Elvis
impersonator.

"Love me tender,"
the goblin croaked
loudly, trying to sing
along.

"He's a terrible
singer!" Rachel
whispered.

"We need to stop
him before someone hears!" Kirsty added
urgently.

"Just be careful, because he can still
freeze us," Rebecca warned as they
zoomed toward the goblin. "But I think
the music has made him forget all about

his freezing powers."

The girls and Rebecca hovered around the goblin's head, but he didn't even notice them until Rebecca tapped him on the shoulder with her wand.

"It's better if you just listen," said Rachel. "Elvis will stop singing if he thinks everyone wants to sing instead of listening to him."

The goblin quieted down immediately. "I don't want him to stop!" He sighed happily.

"Do you like singing?" asked Kirsty.

The goblin nodded. "But goblins aren't any good at singing," he said in a sad voice. "I think it's because we don't have magic singing sticks like the man on the stage."

"Magic singing sticks?" Kirsty questioned.

"Yes, *all* the best singers have them!" the goblin said impatiently. "I've seen them on TV in the human world."

"He means a microphone," Rachel whispered. As she said that, an idea popped into her head. Quickly, she pulled Rebecca and Kirsty aside.

"It's clear that the goblin really wants

to sing like Elvis," she pointed out. "Rebecca, do you think you could use your magic to make a microphone that makes anyone who sings into it sound like Elvis? I'm sure the goblin would trade the magic ribbon for *that*!"

"Of course I can!" Rebecca nodded. "The microphone won't last forever, though. It will dissolve into fairy dust after a few hours."

"That should be long enough," said Rachel. "I'm sure the goblin will have lots of fun with the microphone while it lasts." She swooped down to whisper in the goblin's ear. "Would *you* like to sound like Elvis?" Rachel asked.

The goblin nodded eagerly.

"Well, we can give you a magic singing stick of your very own!" Kirsty said. "Follow us!"

Rebecca and the girls led the goblin away from the stage and into an empty room. First, Rebecca scattered purple fairy dust over Rachel and Kirsty to make them human again. Then, with another flick of her wand, a tall, shining silver microphone appeared in a burst of purple sparkles.

"Oh!" The goblin clapped his hands in delight. "How does it work?"

Rachel went over to the microphone. "You sing into this, and it makes you sound like Elvis," she explained.

Rachel sang *Love Me Tender* into the microphone and was completely surprised

when her voice came out deep and manly, just like Elvis Presley's!

Kirsty and Rebecca laughed.

"Ooh! I want it!" the goblin shrieked excitedly, jumping up and down. "Give me the magic singing stick RIGHT NOW!"

Rockin' Goblin

"We'll swap the magic singing stick for the magic ribbon," Kirsty said. "But you know, this kind of fairy magic doesn't last forever. In a few hours it'll dissolve away into fairy dust."

The goblin barely hesitated. "That's OK," he said, shoving the ribbon at

Rachel and grabbing the microphone stand.

Rebecca gave a little squeal of delight. She immediately shrank the ribbon down to its Fairyland size. It then floated out of Rachel's hand and reattached itself to Rebecca's wand. As it did, the ribbon had a purple glow and lavender sparkles swirled all around it.

Just then, the second goblin rushed into the room.

"He thawed out!" Rachel whispered. "We got the ribbon back just in time!"

The second goblin glared at his friend.

"Why does that pesky fairy have her ribbon back?" he demanded.

"I traded it for this magic singing stick!" the first goblin explained, proudly stroking the silver microphone.

"What?" the second goblin shrieked. "What's Jack Frost going to say when he finds out that you traded the magic ribbon for a silly silver stick?"

"It's not silly!" the first goblin snapped. "Listen!" And he began to sing.

The second goblin looked very impressed when he heard his friend's wonderful Elvis voice. "I want a magic singing stick!" he declared, trying to grab the glittery microphone.

"It's mine!" the first goblin roared. And, picking up the microphone, he

ran off with the other goblin in hot
pursuit.

"I think that's the last we'll see of them
for tonight!" Rebecca laughed. "Girls, I
simply can't thank you enough. You've
been amazing!" She
grinned happily at
Kirsty and Rachel.
"And now I must
go straight back
to Fairyland and
tell everyone the
good news!"

Just then, they heard the sound of
applause from the hall.

"Linda and Will are back onstage,"
Rebecca went on. "And their rock 'n'
roll dance should go well, now that I
have my ribbon back." She waved her

wand at the girls, and the
magic ribbon sparkled.
"Good luck finding the
other ribbons, and
keep a sharp
lookout for
more goblins!"
Rebecca
called. She
vanished in a
cloud of
purple
sparkles as the
girls waved
good-bye.

Kirsty and
Rachel rushed back
into the hall to join
Mr. and Mrs. Tate. They

were just in time to see Will and Linda launch into a very complicated dance routine of steps, kicks, and twists which they performed with perfect timing, neither of them missing a beat. Then Will lifted Linda high over his head. There was a gasp of amazement from the audience as she

jumped right over him and landed
gracefully on the other side.

Rachel and Kirsty grinned at each
other.

"Everything's fine now that Rebecca

has her rock 'n' roll ribbon back,"
Rachel whispered.

"But there are still four more ribbons to
find," Kirsty pointed out with a smile. "I
wonder what our next fairy adventure
will be?"

THE DANCE FAIRIES

Rebecca the Rock 'n' Roll Fairy has her magic ribbon back. Now Rachel and Kirsty need to help

Tasha the Tap Dance Fairy!

Join their next adventure in this special sneak peek!

Tapping Trouble

"Wow," Kirsty Tate said, as she followed her mom through the door of Wetherbury College's main building and saw the crowds inside. "It's really busy in here!"

Her friend, Rachel Walker, who was staying with Kirsty over school break, nodded in agreement. She took off her hat and stuffed it in her pocket as she looked around. "There's a pottery stand," she said, pointing it out. "Ooh, and look, they're decorating cakes over there!"

The girls had come with Kirsty's mom to the college Open House. This was a special event where people could find out more about all the different courses the college offered. Since Mrs. Tate was taking a wood-carving class at the college, she'd volunteered to help out on the wood-working stand and answer any questions people might have. All around the hall there were display tables showing different skills taught at the college.

"There's the wood-carving stand,"

Mrs. Tate said, pointing it out to the girls. "That's where I'll be all morning, OK? But you can wander around and look at everything else. There's lots to see."

Rachel and Kirsty said good-bye and headed off around the room.

"Look!" Kirsty said pointing. "Tap dancers!"

Rachel turned to see. At the far end of the room, some girls in sparkly red tap shoes were practicing a routine. Rachel winced as one of them clumsily dropped her black cane on another dancer's foot. Almost immediately, the girl next to her tripped over it.

"Kirsty, did you see that?" she whispered. "Their dancing is falling apart already!"

Kirsty nodded. "And we both know why," she replied. "It's because Tasha the Tap Dance Fairy's ribbon is still missing!"

Kirsty and Rachel heard a faint tapping sound that was in perfect time to the tap dancers' music.

Tap-tap-tap-tappity-TAP! Tap-tap-tap-tappity-TAP!

Rachel looked over at the dancers eagerly. Did this mean the magic tap dance ribbon was close by, helping the dancers?

But the girls in the sparkly red tap shoes weren't actually dancing at all! *If they're not making the tapping sound, then who is?* Rachel wondered.

RAINBOW magic

THE JEWEL FAIRIES

They Make Fairyland Sparkle!

India the Moonstone Fairy — by Daisy Meadows

Scarlett the Garnet Fairy — by Daisy Meadows

Emily the Emerald Fairy — by Daisy Meadows

Chloe the Topaz Fairy — by Daisy Meadows

Amy the Amethyst Fairy — by Daisy Meadows

Sophie the Sapphire Fairy — by Daisy Meadows

Lucy the Diamond Fairy — by Daisy Meadows

■SCHOLASTIC

www.scholastic.com

www.rainbowmagiconline.com

HiT entertainment

JEWEL

There's Magic in Every Book

The Rainbow Fairies
Books #1-7

The Weather Fairies
Books #1-7

The Jewel Fairies
Books #1-7

The Pet Fairies
Books #1-7

The Fun Day Fairies
Books #1-7

■■SCHOLASTIC
www.scholastic.com
www.rainbowmagiconline.com

HiT entertainment

FAIRY